This book is a gift from

BARNES&NOBLE
BOOKSELLERS

Dear Parent:

Congratulations! Your child is taking
the first steps on an exciting journey.
The destination? Independent reading!

STEP INTO READING® will help your child get there. The program offers
five steps to reading success. Each step includes fun stories and colorful art.
There are also Step into Reading Sticker Books, Step into Reading Math
Readers, Step into Reading Write-In Readers, Step into Reading Phonics
Readers, and Step into Reading Phonics First Steps! Boxed Sets—a complete
literacy program with something for every child.

Learning to Read, Step by Step!

Ready to Read   Preschool–Kindergarten
• big type and easy words • rhyme and rhythm • picture clues
For children who know the alphabet and are eager to
begin reading.

Reading with Help   Preschool–Grade 1
• basic vocabulary • short sentences • simple stories
For children who recognize familiar words and sound out
new words with help.

Reading on Your Own   Grades 1–3
• engaging characters • easy-to-follow plots • popular topics
For children who are ready to read on their own.

Reading Paragraphs   Grades 2–3
• challenging vocabulary • short paragraphs • exciting stories
For newly independent readers who read simple sentences
with confidence.

Ready for Chapters   Grades 2–4
• chapters • longer paragraphs • full-color art
For children who want to take the plunge into chapter books
but still like colorful pictures.

STEP INTO READING® is designed to give every child a successful
reading experience. The grade levels are only guides. Children can progress
through the steps at their own speed, developing confidence in their
reading, no matter what their grade.

Remember, a lifetime love of reading starts with a single step!

Thomas the Tank Engine & Friends®

A BRITT ALLCROFT COMPANY PRODUCTION

Based on The Railway Series by The Reverend W Awdry
Copyright © 2005 Gullane (Thomas) LLC
Thomas the Tank Engine & Friends and Thomas & Friends are trademarks of
Gullane Entertainment Inc.
Thomas the Tank Engine & Friends is Reg. U.S. Pat. TM Off.

A HIT Entertainment Company

All rights reserved under International and Pan-American Copyright Conventions. Published in
the United States by Random House Children's Books, a division of Random House, Inc., and
simultaneously in Canada by Random House of Canada Limited, Toronto.

Illustrated by Richard Courtney

www.stepintoreading.com
www.thomasandfriends.com

Educators and librarians, for a variety of teaching tools, visit us at
www.randomhouse.com/teachers

Library of Congress Cataloging-in-Publication Data
Thomas goes fishing / illustrated by Richard Courtney.
p. cm. — (Step into reading. A step 1 book) "Thomas the tank engine & friends."
Based on The railway series by the Rev. W. Awdry.
"A Britt Allcroft Company production."
SUMMARY: Envious of the children who are fishing in the river near the railroad tracks, Thomas
the tank engine finds a way to enjoy the same activity.
ISBN 0-375-83118-5 (pbk.) — ISBN 0-375-93118-X (lib. bdg.)
[1. Railroads—Trains—Fiction. 2. Fishing—Fiction.] I. Courtney, Richard, ill. II. Awdry, W.
III. Series: Step into reading. Step 1.
PZ7.T36949735 2005   [E]—dc22   2004013892

Printed in the United States of America
First Edition 10 9 8 7 6 5 4 3 2

STEP INTO READING, RANDOM HOUSE, and the Random House colophon are registered trademarks
of Random House, Inc.

WITHDRAWN
Thomas
Goes Fishing

Based on *The Railway Series*
by the Rev. W. Awdry
Illustrated by Richard Courtney

Random House 🏠 New York

Thomas chugged
by the river.
He saw children fishing.

"Peep, peep,"
Thomas said.

6

The children waved.

"I wish to fish,"
said Thomas.

"An engine fishing,"
the Driver said.
"That is funny!"

Each day Thomas
saw the children.
Each day Thomas
wished to fish.

One day
Thomas stopped.

"Oh, dear!" he said.

"My boiler hurts!"

The Driver looked

in the boiler.

It was empty.

The Driver filled
Thomas' boiler
with water
from the river.

Soon they were
chugging along.

Thomas stopped again.
"Hee hee!" said Thomas.

"My boiler feels funny."

The Driver looked
in the boiler.
It was not empty.

There was water
in the boiler.
That was not all!
There were fish, too!

24

Thomas had an idea.
He peeped loudly.
The children came
to see Thomas.

The children could fish
in the river!

The Driver could fish in Thomas!

And that is what
they did.

"Peep! Peep!"